CARROT CHARLIE

CARROT CHARLiE

Monica M Barrett

First paperback edition

Illustrations by Can Ali

Book design by Publishing Push

978-1-80541-010-2 (paperback)

978-1-80541-011-9 (ebook)

Website: mmb-author.my.canva.site

This book is dedicated to my family and friends who have been patient
and continuously encouraged me to pursue my dream of becoming
a published children's author; it's been a long time coming!

Thank you to my extremely talented illustrator, Can Ali.
I look forward to working with you on my other projects.

Lastly, thank you to my readers; I hope you enjoy reading my first
book in the series of Farmer Perry's Fruit and Vegetable Patch.

Happy Reading!

X MMB X

Farmer Perry's Fruit & Vegetable Patch Presents:

CARROT CHARLiE

Carrot Charlie stood tall and strong.

He grew to be five inches long.

He lived deep in a grassy carrot patch,

and was the smoothest carrot

in the whole of the batch.

One sunny day in May,

Carrot Charlie decided to go out and play.

The sun was shining really bright,

so he should be home

before day became night.

As Carrot Charlie bounced along,

he began to hum his favourite song:

As he bounced along, he saw Tutu Turtle.

"Hello Tutu. What's wrong with you?"

Tutu Turtle told Carrot Charlie she wanted to dance

and wanted to dance on a stage in France.

But Tutu Turtle could not see,

and with every twirl she bumped into a tree.

"Hmmm, they say carrots are good for the eyes.

Take a bit. Maybe an inch. Go on, give it a try."

Tutu Turtle took a bite of Carrot Charlie, and with

each munch and delicious crunch, she began to see

that the sky was as blue as the ocean and sea.

"Oh, thank you! Thank you, Charlie.

I can see! I can see!"

"Think nothing of it, Tutu, my friend.

Now you have a chance to dance

on a stage in France.

Remember that you now can see;

try not to bump into those old trees!"

Although he was one inch shorter,

Carrot Charlie bounced on even bolder.

As he bounced along,

he began to hum his favourite song:

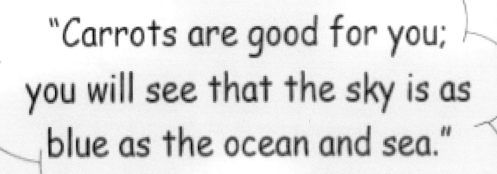

Question: How tall is Carrot Charlie now?

As he bounced along, he saw Fifi Fox.

"Why are you sitting with a frown in that old brown box?"

Fifi explained that she could not see the key for the lock

and she needed to feed her pups before six o'clock.

"Hmmm, they say carrots are good for the eyes.

Take a bit. Maybe an inch. Go on, give it a try."

Question: Can you see Fifi's key?

Fifi Fox took a bite of Carrot Charlie, and with

each munch and delicious crunch, she began to see

that the sky was as blue as the ocean and sea.

"Oh, thank you! Thank you, Charlie.

I can see! I can see the key!"

"Think nothing of it my friend Miss Fox.

Now come away from that old brown box.

Take the key and undo the lock -

feed your pups - it's nearly six o'clock!"

Although he was yet another inch shorter,

Carrot Charlie bounced on even bolder.

As he bounced along,

he began to hum his favourite song:

Question: How tall is Carrot Charlie now?

On his way home, he saw his friend Rafiki Rat.

"Why do you sit trembling, wearing an old, battered hat?"

Rafiki explained that he was as blind as a bat,

and he couldn't see to run away from

Farmer Perry's BIG black cat!

"Hmmm, they say carrots are good for the eyes.

Take a bit. Maybe an inch. Go on, give it a try."

Rafiki Rat took a bite of Carrot Charlie, and with each munch and delicious crunch, he began to see that the sky was as blue as the ocean and sea.

"Oh, thank you! Thank you, Charlie. I can see! That BIG black cat won't be able to catch me."

"You're welcome, Rafiki, my dear friend. Run, run like the wind, and don't look back. Get far away from Farmer Perry's BIG black cat."

Although he was three inches shorter,

Carrot Charlie bounced on even bolder.

As he bounced happily along,

he continued to hum his favourite song:

"Carrots are good for you; you will see that the sky is as blue as the ocean and sea."

Question: How tall is Carrot Charlie now?

That night, before he nestled back into his patch,

Carrot Charlie realised he was now the smallest of the batch.

Before he fell into a comfortable sleep,

Carrot Charlie hoped and prayed

to grow a glorious inch each and every other day.

There are many different ways to eat carrots; why not try some of these:

Carrot sticks

Carrot cake

Carrot soup

Carrot fries

Can you think of any other delicious recipes you can use carrots for?

Why not try making them with your parents/carer;
go on, give it a try!

CARROT
CHARLIE